Midnight Journey

Running for Freedom on the Underground Railroad

By

Shawneen Orzechowski

WHITE MANE KIDS
SHIPPENSBURG, PENNSYLVANIA

This book is a work of historical fiction. Names, characters,
places, and incidents are products of the author's imagination and
are based on actual events.

This White Mane Books publication
was printed by
Beidel Printing House, Inc.
63 West Burd Street
Shippensburg, PA 17257-0708 USA

The acid-free paper used in this book meets the guidelines for
permanence and durability of the Committee on Production Guidelines for Book Longevity of the Council on Library Resources.

For a complete list of available publications
please write
White Mane Books
Division of White Mane Publishing Company, Inc.
P.O. Box 708
Shippensburg, PA 17257-0708 USA

ISBN-10: 1-57249-379-8
ISBN-13: 978-1-57249-379-7

Library of Congress Cataloging-in-Publication Data

Orzechowski, Shawneen, 1971-
  Midnight journey : running for freedom on the Underground
Railroad / by Shawneen Orzechowski.
    p. cm.
  Summary: After Abigail discovers that her parents have been hiding
runaway slaves on their farm, she becomes involved with helping a
young slave girl escape to reunite with her mother.
    ISBN-13: 978-1-57249-379-7 ISBN-10: 1-57249-379-8 (alk. paper)
    1. Underground railroad-Juvenile fiction. [1. Underground railroad-
Fiction. 2. Fugitive slaves-Fiction. 3. Slavery-Fiction.] I. Title.

PZ7.O7845Mid 2005
[Fic]—dc22

                                                        2005045666

Contents

Chapter One
Shadows

Snuggled deep beneath her favorite patchwork quilt, Abigail woke slowly. She opened one hopeful eye, then the other...and groaned.

Through her bedroom window, the sky was already changing from black to lighter shades of blue and gray. In no time at all it would be sunrise. She was late for her chores. Again.

With a sigh, Abigail sat up and threw back the warm quilt, rubbing the last bits of sleep from her eyes. She lit the oil lamp on her bedside table and quickly braided her thick, brown hair. As she buttoned her dress and laced her shoes, however, Abigail noticed that the rest of the house was quiet.

She did not hear the clang of pots and pans as Mama made biscuits and eggs for breakfast. Nor did she hear her mother's quiet humming as she cooked.

Taking the oil lamp to light the way, Abigail tiptoed into the hall. She listened carefully but still heard nothing. Mama must have slept in, too, she realized.

That thought made Abigail smile. After all, if Mama *was* still sleeping, she wouldn't know that Abigail was late for her chores. And if Mama didn't know, Abigail wouldn't be scolded. Besides, Mama needed the rest. She tired so easily now that the baby was almost here.

Abigail stood in the hallway a little longer. Then she dashed to the stairway, trying not to wonder what was hiding in the shadows. She tiptoed down the stairs and hurried out onto the porch, closing the door softly behind her.

Once outside, Abigail shivered. For even though the rains had finally stopped, they had left the morning air cool and damp. Just as she turned back to get her cloak, however, she heard the angry bellows of their cow, Bessie. Bessie didn't like it when anyone was late for her milking.

If her brother, Will, were here, it would have been *his* job to work in the barn, thought Abigail. But Will had gone with Pa to New York three days ago, which had left Abigail to do *all* the chores.

Abigail's thoughts were rudely interrupted by yet another of Bessie's moos.

"I'm coming," Abigail grumbled, kicking a stone into the grass. She held the lamp out high and hurried toward the dark shadow of the barn.

Abigail slowly pulled the barn door open. Inside, it was pitch-black. She stepped in and held out the lamp. Instead of lighting the way, however, the lamp made shadows that jumped and danced in the flickering light.

Before she could lose her nerve, Abigail raced to the far side of the barn.

When she reached Bessie's stall, Abigail set down the lamp and stroked Bessie's head and neck.

"There now. It's all right," she whispered into Bessie's ear, trying to calm herself as much as the bellowing cow.

After Bessie had quieted, Abigail went to fetch the milking stool and bucket in the empty stall beside Bessie's. Though the light from the lamp barely reached inside, Abigail found them easily. But as she started back, a whisper of movement made her skin prickle. Abigail froze. She listened carefully but heard nothing except her own breath, loud and shaky in the silence.

It was only a mouse, she told herself. She had probably scared it when she'd come into the stall.

But then the sound came again, louder this time. Abigail's heart thudded in her ears.

The bucket and stool slipped from her fingers as she spun to her right, planning to run...and came face to face with a hulking form crouched in the shadows. It was a man.

Even in the darkness, she could see the whites of his large, bloodshot eyes.

Abigail screamed. But her scream was cut short as an icy hand came out of the darkness behind her and covered her mouth.

Chapter Two
Discoveries

Abigail struggled and kicked, trying to get away. But the strong hands pulled her back and held tightly. A harsh whisper filled her ear.

"Hush now," it said. "We must not make any noise."

Suddenly, Abigail stopped struggling. That voice. Even in a whisper, she knew that voice. And the scent—Lemon Verbena. Why, it must have been there all along.

Abigail turned. "Mama?"

Abigail's mother nodded. She let go of Abigail's arms.

"Yes, child," she whispered, smoothing her daughter's hair. "It's Mama. It's all right. Now hush."

Before Abigail could say another word, her mother brought the lamp from Bessie's stall and held it high.

"Abigail," she said quietly, "this is Isaac."

Isaac rose slowly from his hiding place. As the light of the flame fell upon him, Abigail gasped. Before her stood a man the color of walnut stain, his dark skin shining with beads of sweat.

Abigail stared, unable to look away. She had never in her life seen anyone like him face to face. And although his arms and face were bruised and scratched, he smiled down at the shadow crouched beside him.

In the light of the lamp, Abigail saw a girl close to her own age hiding behind an old saddle. Her skin, a lighter shade of brown than Isaac's, was also cut and bruised. Her dress, Abigail noticed, was covered in mud and torn badly.

As the girl stood, she stayed close to Isaac. Her eyes darted nervously around the barn.

"Don't worry, Cora," Abigail's mother whispered to her. "You're safe here."

Suddenly, Isaac pressed his hand to his shoulder and closed his eyes tightly. It was then that Abigail noticed the wet, dark stain that had spread from Isaac's left shoulder to his trouser leg. It looked like blood.

Abigail's mother rushed forward and put an arm around his waist. She helped him walk to the back of Bessie's stall.

Cora hurried behind.

Confused, Abigail followed. "Mama, what are you doing?" she asked.

"Please, child, there's no time to talk," her mother whispered. "Isaac is hurt and we must hurry. Clear the hay from the corner and lift the floorboards for me." She laid a hand on her round belly. "It's difficult for me to do it myself."

Abigail simply looked at her mother for a moment. Floorboards? But she did as she was told. Abigail brushed the hay from the corner and found a line of loose boards. One by one, she lifted the boards and propped them against the wall.

When she finished, her eyes widened in surprise. In the light of the lamp, below the missing floorboards, Abigail saw a ladder that led down into a dark room.

Cora climbed down the ladder first, taking the lamp with her. Isaac went next, taking each step slowly. Abigail could see that he was in pain, but he kept moving, never making a sound.

Suddenly, Abigail heard a soft thump outside. In that moment, the barn grew silent. No creaks or groans. No moos or clucks. It was as if the entire barnyard felt an unknown danger and was holding its breath.

Abigail's mother looked toward the door, her finger on her lips. Even in the dark of early morning, Abigail could see the fear in her eyes.

They waited, but heard nothing more. Finally, Abigail's mother was satisfied. She left Bessie's stall and returned moments later with an armful of blankets.

"Abigail, take these down to Isaac and Cora, but be quick."

When Abigail didn't move, her mother glanced toward the barn door again. "Go!" she insisted.

Abigail turned and made her way down the ladder. The room, now dimly lit with the flame of the oil lamp, was small. Three of the walls were made of dirt, the farthest wall of stone.

Isaac and Cora sat in one corner, huddled together.

"Here are some blankets for you," she said quietly, handing them to Cora.

Cora took the blankets and, with Abigail's help, made a bed for Isaac. Then she wrapped the last blanket around her own shoulders to keep warm. "Go on," she told Abigail. "It's not safe for you here. We'll be fine."

Abigail nodded and climbed back up the ladder. As she reached the top, Cora called out her name. When Abigail looked down, she could see tears in Cora's eyes.

"Thank you," Cora said, her voice shaking. "Please...be careful."

Abigail climbed out of the room, replaced the floorboards, and covered the space with hay.

She stood there for a moment, looking at the barn floor. Although Isaac and Cora had the lamp burning in the room below, there was no light shining through into Bessie's stall. Everything looked the same as it always had. But deep down, Abigail knew that nothing would ever be the same again.

Chapter Three
Family Secrets

Abigail's mother was waiting at the barn door when Abigail left Bessie's stall.

"It's not safe to talk now," explained her mother. "Finish milking Bessie and gather the eggs. Then come inside for breakfast. We'll talk there. And, Abigail, finish up quickly. I don't want you to be away from the house for long."

She turned to go, then added, "If you see anyone near the farm, anyone at all, come inside right away."

Abigail finished her chores just as the sun made its way above the treetops. She raced to the house, a basket of eggs in her hand, and burst into the kitchen where her mother was taking golden-colored biscuits out of the oven.

"Mama! Tell me, please!" Abigail exclaimed. She could be patient no longer.

"Abigail, put those eggs down before you break them. And how many times have I told you that a lady does not run?"

"But Mama," Abigail pleaded as she set the basket safely near the wood stove.

"Goodness, child!" her mother sighed. "Sit down a moment and let me think."

From the kitchen table, Abigail watched her mother scoop slabs of ham from the skillet, then add fresh eggs from the basket. She hummed as she worked, but Abigail could tell that she was tired...and worried.

Finally, the eggs finished, Abigail helped her mother make up two breakfast plates. The smell made her mouth water, but she was too excited to eat.

"Abigail," her mother began slowly, "you know that in the South, many people have slaves. For some, slavery is a way of life."

Abigail nodded, her breakfast untouched and growing cold.

"But many others disagree, especially people in the North. They think slavery is wrong—that every person has the right to be free. Some of those people believe in that freedom so strongly, they help slaves to escape, either by traveling to the South and bringing the slaves north or by *hiding* the slaves as they make their journey...like your pa and me."

Abigail's mouth dropped open. "Like you and Pa?" she repeated. She thought of Cora and Isaac in the hidden room below the barn. "Mama, are Cora and Isaac fugitive slaves?" Abigail's eyes sparkled with excitement. She'd often seen WANTED posters for fugitive slaves when they'd visited the general store in town. She'd always wondered how they had escaped, where they went, how they'd stayed hidden for so long. But Abigail had never met a fugitive slave. Never in her whole life!

"Are they, Mama?" she asked again.

"Yes, Abigail, Cora is a fugitive slave. Isaac traveled to South Carolina to help her escape." She frowned, giving Abigail a disapproving look. "But this is not an adventure. What we are doing is serious. And dangerous. Since the Fugitive Slave Act in 1850, hiding fugitive slaves is against the law. No one can know. Not our neighbors, not your friends. Not anyone. Do you understand that, Abigail? Your father and I could go to prison or be fined. We could lose the farm...or worse. Much, much worse."

Abigail stared at her plate. She'd heard a story in town once about a man who was hanged for trying to help a fugitive slave across the New York border to Canada. Could that happen to Pa or Mama? she wondered.

Abigail swallowed and looked up at her mother. "I'll never tell anyone," she promised.

Abigail's mother got up from the table and began packing the leftover biscuits and ham into the egg basket. "This is for Isaac and Cora. I'm sure they haven't had a good meal for days."

"Mama," Abigail asked quietly, "does Will know?"

Her mother sighed deeply. "Abigail, your pa and I didn't want either you or your brother to find out about this until you were older. But yes, I'm afraid he does. You know that, for about two years now, Will has sometimes helped Pa make grain deliveries further north. Some of those deliveries haven't just been grain, Abigail. Sometimes Pa and Will hide the slaves with them in the wagon and take them to their next stop."

"But if Pa and Will are gone, who is going to help Cora and Isaac?"

Abigail's mother took her hands. "We'll just have to keep them safe ourselves until Pa and Will get back.

Isaac is in no shape to make such a dangerous trip anyway. And with the baby coming so soon, I wouldn't dare try. I wouldn't be much help to either Isaac or Cora if I had the baby along the way."

She smiled and touched Abigail's cheek. "Come now, don't look so worried."

But behind the soothing words and smile, Abigail could see that her mother was afraid. She thought of Isaac and Cora, huddled together in the dark, damp room. She remembered their clothing, dirty and torn. And she remembered the blood.

"Mama, why is Isaac bleeding?"

"Isaac was shot," her mother answered evenly, "before he and Cora found our farm."

"Will he be all right?" Abigail asked, worried.

"I hope so. We'll know more soon. In the meantime, I'm going to make him some medicine to try to help him get better."

"But who shot him, Mama?"

"I don't know. But whoever it was could be dangerous. Very dangerous."

Suddenly intense, she grasped Abigail by the shoulders and looked her directly in the eyes. "Listen to me. I want you to stay close to the house unless you are with me. Do you understand?"

"Yes, Mama, but..."

"No buts, Abigail. If Isaac was shot on purpose— and I think he was—the person who shot him could still be near. As long as he's near, no one is safe. Not Isaac or Cora. Not me. And not you."

Chapter Four
Medicine for Isaac

After Abigail had drawn water from the well, she sat down at the kitchen table. She loved to watch her mother make medicine.

Abigail's mother stoked the fire in the stove to make it hotter, then took a bottle of whiskey from the cupboard. She poured some whiskey into a small pan sitting on the stove. Next, she scooped a smaller amount of water from the bucket and added it to the whiskey. After a while, it began to boil.

She was making a tincture, if Abigail remembered the word correctly. Abigail had watched her mother make tinctures before, for all kinds of ailments such as colds and cuts and bruises. All of the tinctures had both water and some kind of alcohol in them. But then her mother would add special healing ingredients, like herbs, roots or flowers.

Abigail's mother opened another cupboard and took out a small jar.

"What is it, Mama?" Abigail asked, looking at the powder inside the jar.

"It's dried calendula, pounded into a powder."

"You mean the flowers we planted in front of our house? But what will they do?"

Abigail's mother opened the jar as she spoke. "Calendula will help to heal Isaac's wound more quickly. It will also help to stop the bleeding and, hopefully, prevent gangrene."

She took out a square of cheesecloth and scooped calendula powder onto the center.

"May I help, Mama?"

Abigail's mother nodded. "Make the cheesecloth into a little sack. Then we'll dip the sack into the liquid."

Abigail gathered the corners of the cheesecloth and tied them with string. Then, holding on to the string, she lowered the sack into the boiling liquid. The sack bobbed back and forth as she held it. Every now and then, her mother would tell her to pull the sack out of the water to let it drain, then hold it under again.

As Abigail stood at the stove, watching the ingredients become Isaac's medicine, she crinkled her nose. "It doesn't smell very good."

Her mother laughed. "Not everything that's good for you actually smells good, you know."

Abigail thought of the horrible onion poultice that her mother had made her wear the last time she was sick. She crinkled her nose again. "I know. I know."

After a long time, her mother checked the liquid and the calendula sack. "Well, it should really boil longer, but this will have to do. We need to get this medicine to Isaac quickly." She squeezed the sack until all the liquid was gone and set it aside. Then she took the pan from the stove.

"Abigail, get me two more squares of cheesecloth from the cupboard, please."

Abigail handed the pieces of cheesecloth to her mother and watched as she placed them in the pan. The cheesecloth soaked up the medicine quickly.

While her mother gathered strips of cloth for Isaac's wound, Abigail folded the medicine-soaked cheesecloth and put it into a small bowl. She then packed the bowl, the last of the ham, and biscuits into the bottom of the basket. She covered it all with a handkerchief, then set the unused eggs on top. If anyone came by while she and her mother were on the way to the barn, it would look like they had just been gathering eggs in the hen house.

* * * * *

Abigail looked carefully through the kitchen window. As far as she could tell, the yard was empty. Satisfied that they would be safe, Abigail and her mother went outside, drew fresh water from the well, and walked to the barn, the food and medicine carefully hidden away.

Once inside, they went directly to Bessie's stall and knocked on the floor. Abigail lifted the boards and set them aside. In the dim light below, she saw Cora already waiting. She handed the food basket and water pail down to Cora, then helped her mother down the ladder. It was a tight fit with her mother's belly so big and round.

"Isaac is feeling worse," whispered Cora, once they were safely in the room. "I wish we could get a doctor."

"I'm afraid that's not possible yet," said Abigail's mother. "But I've made up some medicine myself."

She knelt down beside Isaac and, with Cora's help, gently removed his shirt.

Isaac groaned softly but remained still.

Next, Abigail's mother dipped a cloth into the water bucket and cleaned away the dirt and blood from his wound.

Isaac sat back and closed his eyes. Each time her mother wiped, Isaac clenched his hand into a fist and took long, deep breaths.

Though she stayed back to give her mother room to work, Abigail was fascinated. She'd seen plenty of cuts and scrapes before, many of them her own. But she'd never seen a bullet wound.

The bullet had gone all the way through Isaac's shoulder, from front to back. The hole it had left was ragged. The edges were swollen and red.

"I've made you some medicine. It should help the wound heal properly and stop the bleeding," Abigail's mother told Isaac.

She laid one section of cheesecloth on the front of Isaac's shoulder and another on the back, then held them in place with strips of cloth wrapped securely around his shoulder.

She turned to Cora. "You'll need to watch Isaac closely today. I'll check his shoulder later and bring him more medicine. Until then, you both should try to eat and get plenty of rest."

As Isaac and Cora began to eat, Abigail said, "Isaac, Mama told me that someone shot you."

Isaac nodded and placed his hand on Cora's. "Cora and I were headed north, on our way to Jenkins' Falls when we came across Thomas Blake, a slave catcher who has been tracking us since we traveled through Virginia. I've heard plenty about him. None of it good. He's a cruel man and a good tracker—one of the best, in fact. The worst part is, he loves his job. And he's paid well for doing it."

Isaac lay down on his makeshift bed.

"Luckily we saw Blake before he saw us," he continued, "but we had to travel west to get away from him. When Blake did find us, it was difficult to see because of the storm—which is why I was only shot in the shoulder. It could have been—would have been—worse.

"The bullet hit me hard and threw me back, but Cora thought quickly and helped pull me into the underbrush."

Isaac stopped and smiled at Cora.

"With the rain and thunder booming overhead, Blake didn't hear us. In fact, he walked right past our hiding place. He must have thought we'd gotten away. When we were sure he was gone, we kept walking. It was difficult, but with Cora's help, we ended up here."

"Do you think he'll try to find you again?" Abigail's mother asked.

Isaac nodded. "Yes. He knows we're in the area. A man like Blake won't stop until he finds us."

"Well, I think you'll be safe here," said Abigail's mother, getting ready to leave. "Stay as long as you need to."

Isaac sat up and groaned with pain. "We're thankful for your kindness." He paused and closed his eyes. "But we have to leave tonight when it turns dark. It's too dangerous for us, and for you, if we stay."

Abigail's mother turned and scolded, "You will do no such thing, Isaac. You are in no shape to travel."

"But if I know Thomas Blake," said Isaac, "he'll be back. No one is safe until Cora and I are gone."

Chapter Five
Daydreams

"Abigail, you're supposed to knead the dough, not just slide it back and forth on the table."

Startled, Abigail looked up to see her mother standing in the kitchen, her hand resting neatly on her belly.

"You surprised me!" she exclaimed. "I didn't even hear you come in."

"It's no wonder," her mother laughed. "You're in your own little world. What were you daydreaming about?"

Abigail looked down at the dough she'd been working on for the last twenty minutes. It was still wet and sticky.

"Sorry, Mama. I've been thinking about Isaac and Cora. I can't seem to think about anything else."

"I know." Abigail's mother walked over and kissed her cheek. "Why don't you wash your hands and go upstairs to read for a while. I know you've been wanting to finish that book of yours. Maybe it will get your mind off of all that's happened today. I'll make the bread."

* * * * *

Abigail tried. But reading her book turned out to be just as useless as making the bread. She couldn't read more than a paragraph without her mind drifting. Her thoughts always turned to Cora.

She and Cora were around the same age, Abigail thought. And here she was, lying on her comfortable bed, reading a book, while Cora was hiding in a small, damp room, sitting on a dirt floor, running for her freedom...and possibly her life. Abigail couldn't even imagine what it must be like.

Cora had been very quiet both times Abigail had seen her. She'd looked so tired and scared. But underneath it all, how brave she must be!

And what does Cora think about during the days while she's hidden away? Abigail wondered. Does she think about the place she'd left and the people she knew? Does she think about what she'll be and what she'll do when she's free? And what about her family? Abigail felt that she needed to do something to help, but what?

Then she had a thought. Isaac and Cora would probably be here for at least a few more days, until Isaac was well enough to leave. And even though Cora was taking care of Isaac, she must be bored, with nothing to do but sit and worry when Isaac was asleep.

"I'll bet Cora would like this book as much as I do," she said to herself. "I'll bring it to her the next time Mama checks on Isaac."

With that decision came a small comfort. Although it wasn't much, at least she was doing *something* to make Cora feel better.

Abigail dove into the pages of her book, barely noticing her mother's soft humming and the heavenly smell of baking bread.

Chapter Six
Thomas Blake

Just as Abigail turned to the last chapter of her book, a loud knock on the front door made her jump.

Seconds later, it came again.

She ran to the top of the stairs, heart pounding. Just then, her mother passed by the stairway on her way to the door, wiping her hands on her apron.

She looked up at Abigail and put her finger to her lips.

Abigail nodded.

Though she couldn't see the door from her hiding place at the top of the stairs, Abigail could hear her mother clearly. She heard the door open. Then, for a few long seconds, there was silence. Abigail wished she could see what was happening.

Finally, her mother spoke.

"Yes," she said politely. "Can I help you?"

"Hello, ma'am," boomed a deep, Southern voice.

Abigail's heart pounded in her ears. It was a man's voice. Was it *his*? Was it Thomas Blake's?

"Nice day," he continued. "Although I do see some dark clouds rolling in. Looks like it may rain again tonight."

"Yes, there does seem to be another storm on the way," her mother agreed.

Abigail was torn between staying upstairs as she'd been told or getting a better look at the man standing in their doorway. Her curiosity won.

Abigail crept down two steps, leaned over as far as she could...and gasped.

In the doorway stood one of the biggest men Abigail had ever seen. He towered an entire head, shoulders, and chest above her mother. His shoulders were so wide they nearly touched the insides of the doorway. He'd politely taken off his hat and held it in one hand, but in the other, he carried a rifle.

"Can I help you?" her mother repeated.

"Ma'am, my name is Thomas Blake. I'm looking for a runaway slave, a young girl around the age of fifteen." He took a sheet of paper from his pocket and handed it to her. "Her name is Cora. This paper will tell you a little more about her.

"I'm sure she's in the area," he continued as Abigail's mother read Cora's description. "I tracked her and a man to these parts not long ago. The man might be wounded—they couldn't have gotten far."

Abigail panicked. Isaac and Cora, she thought. He knows they're here. She wanted to warn them. But how? The only way to get to the barn was to go down the steps and out the door. And she couldn't do that.

"Have you seen them, ma'am?" Blake asked.

Abigail's mother looked up from the paper. "No, Mr. Blake," she said, "I haven't."

Wanting to get a closer look, Abigail crept down one more step. But as she put her weight on it, it let out a startling groan.

Abigail's breath caught in her throat. She closed her eyes. Maybe they hadn't heard...

"Ma'am," Blake said, "are you sure you haven't seen the two I'm looking for?" He pushed past Abigail's mother, taking his rifle in both hands.

"Well, who have we here?"

Abigail opened her eyes to find Blake standing at the bottom of the stairs, his rifle raised, looking at her.

"Come on down, miss," he said. "No reason to be afraid."

But Abigail was afraid. Very afraid. She took each step slowly until she was a couple of steps from the bottom.

"Abigail, sweetheart," her mother interrupted, "this is Mr. Blake." She stepped forward, placing herself between Abigail and the rifle, and held out her hand. "He was asking me some questions."

Grateful, Abigail went to her mother's side, took her hand, and held tight.

Blake put down the rifle and looked at Abigail.

Abigail's mother squeezed her hand, silently telling her not to be afraid. But when Blake leaned closer, Abigail wanted to run.

"Abigail, is it?" he asked.

She stammered, "Y-Yes sir."

"Abigail, I'm looking for a runaway slave named Cora. Have you seen anyone like that around here?" He stared at her, waiting for an answer, his eyes half closed in a scowl. He was so close she could see a faint scar along his left cheek and smell the strong odor of onion on his breath.

"No sir," she answered quietly, hoping he'd go away.

But Blake simply stood and picked up his rifle. "Mind if I look around?" he asked.

It wasn't a question, really, Abigail noticed. He was already beginning to search the kitchen.

"Of course," said her mother calmly.

Abigail knew her mother didn't have a choice. If she had refused, Blake would have been suspicious. But it seemed as though Blake wasn't about to let them refuse.

As Abigail and her mother stood helplessly by the stairs, Thomas Blake looked around the kitchen—under the table, inside the cupboards, and even inside the cooling wood stove.

Next, he walked into the parlor, his eyes moving everywhere for a trace of Cora and Isaac or their hiding place. Finding nothing in her mother's cabinet, under and behind the furniture, or inside the fireplace, he moved slowly up the stairs to the rooms above.

Abigail and her mother heard his footsteps tramping through one bedroom after the other.

"He won't find anything, Abigail," her mother whispered. "It will be all right."

When he came back down into the kitchen, Abigail's mother said boldly, "Mr. Blake, we've allowed you to search our home. As I said, we haven't seen your runaway slave. Now if you'll excuse us, we have work to do."

"Of course."

Thomas Blake opened the door. He turned and added, "They're in the area. If you see them, let me know." He looked Abigail's mother directly in the eyes and lowered his voice in warning. "I'll be in the area, too."

Chapter Seven
Blake Again

Abigail stood at the kitchen window, watching Thomas Blake as he mounted his horse and rode away. Certain he was gone, Abigail hurried to the barn, directly to Bessie's stall.

She scratched Bessie's head for a moment, talking to her quietly. Bessie nuzzled her nose into Abigail's dress and mooed.

With a giggle, Abigail hugged Bessie's neck. "Be a good girl now, Bessie."

Just as she was about to clear the hay from the corner of the stall, that same deep voice caught her attention.

"Well, Miss Abigail, we meet again."

Abigail whirled toward him. "Oh, Mr. Blake. You startled me."

Abigail calmed herself by giving Bessie one last rub. Then, thinking quickly, she complained, "I have so many more chores to do since my brother left." She found an unfinished chore far from the stall and began to work.

"Will usually does the barn chores," she chatted on, trying to draw his attention away from Bessie's stall...and away from Isaac and Cora.

But it didn't work.

"Nice size cow you have here," Blake said, walking over to Bessie. He gave her a pat.

Bessie mooed loudly, shuffling her feet.

"Be careful," Abigail warned. "Bessie doesn't like strangers."

Ignoring Abigail's warning, Blake laughed and patted Bessie's side once more. Upset by the stranger, Bessie's moos turned to angry bellows.

Abigail's mother rushed through the barn door.

"Abigail, what are you doing out here? What's wrong with..." She stopped in mid-sentence. "Mr. Blake!"

"Just taking another look around, ma'am," he said. "Seems like you're a nice enough woman. I wouldn't want those slaves wandering onto your property and thinking they could hide here without your knowledge. I've had a look around your barn. It looks safe. But..."

Looking down at the hay at the back of Bessie's stall, he stopped. "Well, what do we have here? It looks like blood."

Blake bent over to look more closely at three reddish-black spots on the hay next to Bessie.

An image of Isaac's bloody shirt popped into Abigail's mind. The blood must have dripped onto the hay when Isaac and Cora were in Bessie's stall. Her mind raced.

"I cut myself on a nail in Bessie's stall yesterday," Abigail lied. "It bled a lot. But Mama took care of it."

"Is that so?" Thomas Blake asked. "I'll take a look at the cut if you'd like. You can't be too careful with those things."

Just then, to Abigail's relief, Bessie stomped her feet, moving around angrily in the stall. With one final moo, she bumped into Blake.

Still bent over and quite off balance, Blake fell, stomach first, into a pile of fresh manure.

He pushed himself up quickly.

"No-account cow," he yelled, and raised his foot to give Bessie a hard, swift kick.

"Oh, Mr. Blake," Abigail's mother cried before he could hurt the cow. "Your shirt! Please come with me. I'll wash it right away."

"Forget it," he fumed, walking toward the barn door. "She's not here. But she's close. And I'll find her, be sure of that. After all, she's just a girl."

He stormed out, slamming the door.

After making sure he was really gone this time, Abigail ran to Bessie's stall and quickly raked up the bloody hay.

She turned to Bessie and gave her a hug. "That was close, Bessie," she laughed. "You really are a good girl. And smart, too. You knew just what to do."

Chapter Eight
The Decision

Abigail and her mother kept a close watch throughout the rest of the day. But even as the sun made its way across the late afternoon sky, Thomas Blake did not return.

Abigail giggled as they stepped into Bessie's stall. She could still see the look on Blake's face when he'd fallen into the fresh manure.

She went to the corner and knocked quietly on the floor. After one more quick look around, she pushed the hay aside, removed the boards and climbed down the ladder.

The lantern in the small room was burning. In its dim light, Abigail saw Isaac lying on his bed of blankets. Cora leaned over him, talking softly.

"How is he?" Abigail asked.

"He's sleeping, but he has a fever," Cora whispered, wiping Isaac's forehead.

Abigail took Isaac's hand. It was hot and sweaty.

"Mama has more medicine for him. She's up above, keeping watch while I'm down here. I'll get her now."

Abigail climbed up the ladder and disappeared.

She found her mother looking anxiously out the barn window.

"Mama," she whispered, pulling on her arm, "Isaac is sick. Cora says he has a fever. You need to come. Now."

After one last look outside, Abigail's mother hurried toward the opening in the floor, the medicine-soaked cheesecloth wrapped and hidden in the pockets of her skirt.

As before, her round stomach made the climb down difficult. But with help, she was soon kneeling beside Isaac.

When she removed the old bandages, Isaac opened his eyes.

"Is it safe for you to be down here?" he asked.

"I think so." She paused. "Isaac, I know you had planned on leaving tonight, but you can't. You're too weak and too sick. We may not have gotten the medicine on soon enough. You could never walk to Jenkins' Falls, especially with Thomas Blake so near."

"I'll be fine," he argued. "Blake was right above us today. The longer we're here, the longer we're all at risk. Besides, Cora's mother is waiting. We're leaving tonight."

Quiet until now, Cora spoke up. "Isaac, she's right. You're too sick to go anywhere. You've done so much for me already. Don't worry, I'll find my mother somehow."

"Find your mother?" Abigail asked. "What do you mean?"

Cora shook her head. She kept her eyes on the floor as she spoke. "I was taken from my mother and sold when I was about eight years old. My mother has been trying to find me all this time. Now she's waiting for me. Isaac's going to help me find her."

Cora wiped away a small tear that had spilled down her cheek.

Abigail sat down beside Cora. She put an arm around her shoulders. "You'll get to her, Cora," she said. "I know you will."

"Yes, she will," Isaac promised. He reached over to put a fevered hand on Cora's. "I'll make sure she does."

Abigail's mother replaced Isaac's old, dried pieces of cheesecloth with the new ones, wrapping them tightly once again. She shook her head. "Isaac, in the thunderstorm, after you were shot, you wandered far from Jenkins' Falls. It's miles from here. In your condition, there's no way you can make it. Stay here until you're well."

Isaac winced in pain. "Miles?" His shoulders slumped forward. "No, I still have to try. Cora is my responsibility."

"When you're better, you can take her. But until then, Isaac, you and Cora both need time."

Isaac rubbed a hand over his face and sighed. "Unfortunately, time is something we don't have," he argued. "It's taken us longer than I thought it would to get this far north. Cora should already have been in Jenkins' Falls. She would have been if it hadn't been for Blake. But now we don't have time to rest."

Abigail's mother took Isaac's hand. "Isaac, couldn't you go later, after you're well? Why is it important to reach Jenkins' Falls so soon?"

"The people who are helping us in Jenkins' Falls," Isaac explained, "are the same ones who helped Cora's mother. They were going to take us to a family in Hadley that knows where Cora's mother is. But it takes several days to get from Jenkins' Falls to Hadley. And, unfortunately, people in Hadley are starting to get suspicious. So Cora's mother has to move on or risk getting caught. That means the latest Cora can leave from Jenkins' Falls is early tomorrow morning. Otherwise, we won't get to Cora's mother in time. And we'll have no idea where she's gone."

Isaac laid his head down on the blankets. Cora wiped his forehead with a cloth.

"I may die from this bullet wound," Isaac continued.

"Isaac, I don't want to hear talk like that," scolded Abigail's mother.

"I apologize, ma'am, but it needs to be said. If I die, then Cora needs to be on that wagon. She won't know where to go by herself. She won't know which people to trust. The folks in Jenkins' Falls will take care of her. They'll help her find her mother."

"But you said that Cora would need to be there by tomorrow morning, Isaac."

Finding strength in his decision, Isaac sat up. "Cora *is* going to be in Jenkins' Falls by morning. I am going to find a way to get her there."

Abigail's mother took Isaac by the arms and gently laid him back down.

She looked at Cora. "I'll take her," she began before Isaac could argue further. "Abigail can stay here and take care of you."

Abigail had wandered across the room, only half listening to the argument between Isaac and her mother. She couldn't imagine what it would be like to be taken from her own mother and not be able to see her for years. But her mother's words interrupted her thoughts.

"Mama, you can't!" exclaimed Abigail. She looked down at her mother's bulging belly. "Pa and Will have taken our wagon. You'd have to walk! And the baby could come at any time. You said so yourself."

At that moment, a thought came to Abigail. She knew what had to be done.

Abigail walked over to where Cora was sitting. She put her hand on Cora's shoulder. "I'll take her, Mama!"

The arguing stopped. A heavy silence filled the air as everyone stared at Abigail.

"You will do no such thing, young lady!" her mother scolded. "You don't understand how dangerous this is."

"Mama, Isaac can't take her," Abigail insisted. "He's hurt. You can't take her either, not with the baby. But I can. I know my way to Jenkins' Falls. And Cora just has to get there, Mama.

"Besides, Isaac needs your help. I wouldn't know what to do about the medicine. I wouldn't be able to help him very much on my own."

She turned to Isaac. "Please let me go. Cora has to be in that wagon tomorrow morning. She needs to see her mother again. I know I'd do anything to see my mother if I was the one who had been taken away."

Isaac smiled. With great effort, he sat up and took Abigail's hand. To her mother, he said, "This is a brave girl you've raised. You should be proud. Let her help."

For a long moment, Abigail's mother said nothing. She looked at Isaac, then at Cora's and Abigail's hopeful faces. She knew they were right. Someone had to get Cora to Jenkins' Falls.

She shut her eyes tightly and nodded. "All right, Abigail, you may go."

Cora and Abigail threw their arms around her.

"Thank you, ma'am," Cora whispered behind a fountain of tears. "Don't you worry. We'll be safe. I won't let anything happen to Abigail."

Abigail's mother smiled. Then she kissed each girl on the forehead. "Well, both of you need to rest. You have a long night ahead of you."

"Yes ma'am," they both replied.

Cora sat down beside Isaac once again, pulling the heavy blanket around her.

Abigail followed as her mother climbed slowly up the ladder. When Abigail got to the top, however, she stopped.

"Cora, I almost forgot," she whispered. She reached into her skirt pocket and pulled out her book. "With everything that's happened, I almost didn't give you this."

"What is it?" asked Cora.

"It's a book. It's my favorite. I thought you might want to keep it with you and read it while you're hiding. You must be bored and it will take your mind off Thomas Blake."

She climbed back down the ladder and handed the book to Cora.

Cora took the book and smiled. "Thank you, Abigail," she said quietly. "I'll take good care of it."

"I know. I'll see you soon."

With that, Abigail climbed the ladder and disappeared into the barn above.

Chapter Nine
Waiting

Alone in her bedroom, Abigail stood looking out her window. The sun had already set. Little by little, the pale blue sky grew darker. What an amazing day it had been.

Soon, she thought. When the sky turned fully black, when they could walk under the cover of darkness, she and Cora would leave the farm.

As she lit the oil lamp, she heard a knock on the door. Abigail's mother peeked in.

"Abigail," she scolded, "you're supposed to be resting!"

Abigail rolled her eyes. "Resting? How could I possibly rest?"

Seeing the excitement in her daughter's eyes, she smiled. "I know. Well, it's too late for that now, anyway. It's time to get ready."

She handed Abigail a stack of neatly folded clothes.

"What's this?" Abigail asked.

"Your clothes for tonight."

Abigail held up a pair of brown trousers, a dark blue shirt, and a hat.

"But these are boys' clothes," she complained.

Her mother nodded. "They're Will's old clothes. He's outgrown them, but they should fit you just fine. I have some for Cora, too."

"But Mama, why do we have to dress like boys?"

Abigail's mother took her hand. They sat on the bed.

"Thomas Blake has seen you, Abigail. He knows what Cora looks like, too. Hopefully he's not still in the area, at least not close, but if he is, it will be safer for the two of you if you're in disguise. If Blake happens to see you tonight and you're dressed like a boy, he may not recognize you.

"Besides, the clothing is dark and hard to see at night. And sneaking through the woods will be much easier if you're wearing trousers instead of a dress.

"Come now. It's time to go to the barn. And we have food and clothing to pack."

Chapter Ten
In Disguise

Abigail and her mother slipped into the barn, each carrying a bucket full of food and clothing. After a quick look around, they knocked on the floorboards in Bessie's stall and started down.

It had been completely dark but when Cora heard the quiet knock, she lit the lantern, then hurried to the ladder to help Abigail's mother.

Once they were all in the room, with the boards above safely back in place, they began to prepare.

While Abigail's mother took care of Isaac's wound and tried to get him to eat, Abigail and Cora changed into Will's clothes. They giggled as they dressed.

But Abigail's giggles stopped suddenly when she saw Cora's back and legs in the dim light. They were covered with dark, raised lines. At least a dozen, some straight across, others crisscrossed. What were they? she wondered. Then she knew. Scars. "Oh, Cora!" Abigail reached out her hand to comfort her new friend.

But Cora pulled away and dressed quickly, covering herself with Will's shirt and trousers. Abigail pulled back her hand and said nothing more. What could she say, after all? Nothing would take away those scars or the hurt.

Then Cora turned and took Abigail's hands in her own. She smiled and laughed. Cora's laugh was infectious. So Abigail pushed the horrible thoughts from her mind and giggled as she looked at Cora in Will's clothes.

Abigail wished that she could see herself, too. Being in boys' clothing felt so odd. It was as if she were a completely different person.

"How do I look?" Abigail asked Cora.

"Like a boy with long hair and braids," she replied. "You forgot to put on the hat."

Cora twisted Abigail's braids into a knot on the top of her head, then placed the hat over it.

"Perfect," she said proudly, pulling the brim down to the top of Abigail's ears. "Your own father wouldn't recognize you."

Next, Abigail helped Cora. She straightened her clothes and covered her hair with a hat similar to her own. Will's trousers were a little too big on Cora, so Abigail tucked them neatly into Cora's boots.

"Wow," said Abigail. "You look so different!"

"Just call me Alexander," Cora stated, hands on her hips, feet planted wide apart.

They broke into giggles again.

"All right you two," Abigail's mother called. "Enough. Come over here beside Isaac. We want to talk to you about tonight."

In a voice that was barely a whisper, Isaac spoke to them about the night ahead.

"Abigail," he asked, "are you certain you know how to get to Jenkins' Falls?"

"Yes," she answered. "I've been there before with Ma, Pa, and Will."

"But that was by road." He looked back and forth between Abigail and Cora. "Tonight you won't be able to use the road. You'll have to stay as far away from roads and houses—as far away from other people—as you can."

He turned to Cora. "Just like we've been doing."

Cora nodded.

"It will take longer to go through the woods," he continued, "but if you keep a good pace with only a few short rests, you should be able to make it by sunrise."

Abigail squeezed Cora's hand and nodded. "We will."

"I hope so," said Isaac. "But if something slows you down and you're still in the woods at sunrise, stay in the woods. Find a place to hide and rest until night comes again. Then try to make your way back here."

Isaac stopped talking for a moment and closed his eyes. He placed a hand over his bandages and breathed deeply.

"Cora, you know how to find a good hiding place—just in case."

"Yes, Isaac," she nodded.

"All right. Now listen carefully. Both of you."

He looked at Cora, then Abigail.

"On your way to Jenkins' Falls, talk as little as possible. You may not see or hear another person tonight, but if you do, you don't want *them* to see or hear *you*.

"The hardest part will be when you get to Jenkins' Falls. It will be close to morning and the sky will be getting lighter. That means it will be easier for someone to see you.

"Do you remember seeing the mill in town when you were there before, Abigail?"

"Yes," she answered, "I think so."

"Good. Try to get to the mill by going *around* the town if you can, not *through* it. Behind the mill you'll see a white farmhouse on the hill. There will be a candle burning in the top left window. That candle is one of the signals that means runaway slaves, like Cora, are welcome.

"Do you understand so far?"

Abigail and Cora looked at each other and nodded.

"When you find the house, check the area carefully. Make sure no one sees you. Then Abigail will go to the door. When someone asks you who you are, say 'A friend with friends.'"

"A friend with friends?" Abigail asked, confused.

Isaac explained. "'A friend with friends' is a phrase we use to let someone know we're helping a fugitive slave and need a place to hide.

"The folks in Jenkins' Falls will give you food and a safe place to rest. They will help take Cora to her mother and get you back to your mother, too, Abigail."

He shivered. Abigail could see the goosebumps on his skin under a layer of shiny sweat.

She placed her hand on his arm and could feel the heat of his fever. Though he fought it, his eyes were slowly closing.

"Don't worry about me. I'll be fine."

Abigail's mother got up. With tears in her eyes, she looked at each girl in turn. "I can't believe how different you look," she said softly.

She walked to the opposite corner of the room, her arms wrapped around herself. "I have food in the buckets for your journey," she said, her voice shaking. "Put some in this knapsack so you can take it with you."

She turned toward them. "Well, even though I don't like it, it's time for you to go."

Chapter Eleven
The Tunnel

Abigail's mother walked over to the far stone wall.

"Girls, help me move these crates of carrots and potatoes," she whispered.

Together, they moved three large crates, stacking them neatly in a corner.

When they were finished, Abigail gasped. Built neatly into the stone wall, hidden by the crates, stood a wooden door. It was small and square, only big enough to crawl through.

Abigail's stomach fluttered.

"Are you sure you want to do this?" her mother asked, tucking a loose strand of hair back under Abigail's hat.

Abigail nodded and hugged her mother fiercely.

"You can do it," Isaac whispered faintly from his bed. "You're two of the bravest girls I've met. Together, you can do it."

Exhausted from talk, worry, and sickness, Isaac's eyes started to drift shut once again. But before he fell asleep, he looked over at Cora. "Say hello to your mother for me."

Abigail smiled at the thought. Her butterflies disappeared. They *could* do this. They *would* do this. Cora was going to get to Jenkins' Falls. Abigail would do anything she had to do in order to make it happen.

Abigail's mother opened the small door. Beyond the opening, Abigail could see nothing but blackness.

"We're going in there?" she asked.

Her mother nodded. "It's just a tunnel. It leads into the woods on the edge of our property. If anyone is outside, they won't see you leave the barn."

She touched Abigail's cheek. "I'll go first since I have the lantern."

Though it was difficult, she crawled through the tight space, into the darkness.

"Your turn, Cora," she whispered when she was inside.

Cora quickly wrapped the book that Abigail had given her in clean, dry linen, slipped it into the waistband of her trousers, and crawled through.

Abigail followed, carrying the knapsack.

The first thing Abigail noticed when she entered the tunnel was the strong odor of dirt and dampness.

"It smells in here," she complained, crinkling up her nose.

In the lamp's dim light, she looked around the tunnel. It was narrow and low, the walls and ceiling made of roughly dug dirt. She could see shovel and pick marks and imagined her father down here, late at night, digging in the dim light.

The floor of the tunnel was also made of dirt, but unlike the rough walls, the floor was smooth from wear. Without being told, she knew. Many people had walked here.

As she followed her mother, Abigail saw a stray handprint here and there, set into the rough dirt walls. Some were the large prints of adults. Others had been made by children even younger than she and Cora.

How many slaves had walked this very tunnel with the dream of being free? Abigail wondered, placing her hand over one of the prints.

After what felt like minutes, they stopped.

Here, the tunnel widened.

"We're at the end," her mother said, placing the lantern on the floor near a ladder. She gathered the girls close and kissed each one on the cheek.

She wiped the tears from her face and turned toward the ladder.

"There's a door at the top of the ladder," she explained. "Push it up slowly and peek out first. We don't want any surprises."

Before Abigail could go up, her mother pulled her aside. "Abigail, you'll have to cross Maple Creek if you travel through the woods. In some places it's wide and very dangerous."

"Yes," Abigail assured her. "I know just where to cross."

"You do?"

Abigail nodded. "Will used to take me there sometimes. We found a way to cross on the stones. In one spot, the creek gets narrow and the stones almost make a bridge."

"But it's dark. The stones will be hard to see. Please be careful!"

While her mother held the lamp high, Abigail climbed the ladder and pushed gently on the door. She heard the crinkle of leaves and the scrape of a branch against its wooden planks.

In the silence of the night, the noise seemed to echo. She stopped and waited, then pushed the door open an inch further and peeked out.

Abigail saw the trunks of trees around her and, in the distance, a treeless area that must have been the farm. Otherwise, she was alone.

"It's all right," she whispered.

She pushed harder on the door and climbed out with Cora behind her.

From inside the tunnel, Abigail's mother looked out, tears shining brightly in her eyes. "Please be safe," she whispered. "And Abigail, I love you."

Chapter Twelve
Time to Go

Abigail quietly slid the cover back over the tunnel opening. She covered it with leaves and fallen branches until it was well hidden.

Even though she knew her mother was just a few feet away, Abigail suddenly felt alone. Alone in the world. Alone in the darkness. And far from home.

She took Cora's hand. Together, they huddled silently among the trees at the edge of the woods.

Sounds of the night surrounded them. Crickets chirped. Wings fluttered and flapped. An owl hooted. And once, a small creature scurried through the underbrush, making them jump.

But as one long minute stretched into the next, they decided that they were alone.

Abigail looked at Cora. Cora said nothing, but nodded in agreement. It was time to go.

They stood slowly. Although Abigail knew these woods and had played in them all of her life, she'd never been in the woods at night, without a lantern. Now everything seemed so different. The trees looked like people standing very still. She imagined their wide branches to be arms, reaching out to grab her.

To make matters worse, heavy clouds now blanketed the sky above. As a result, the moon, which should have been full and bright, offered little light.

Abigail concentrated.

Finally, as she looked to her left, she noticed a familiar, dark shape in the distance. The barn.

In that instant, a renewed feeling of hope flooded through her. She knew exactly where they were and, more importantly, which way to go.

Chapter Thirteen
Footsteps in the Dark

Though it was more difficult in darkness, Abigail found the small path she and Will had made long ago. If she could keep to it without losing her way, they would make it to the creek in close to an hour.

The path was well-worn, winding around trees and rocks, deeper into the forest. Though Abigail remembered the way clearly, roots and stumps, almost invisible in the dark, made travel slow.

They walked carefully, testing their footing before each step. Even still, they were poked, scraped, and bruised by overgrown bushes and branches that reached out over the path.

But Abigail, her mind on Thomas Blake, barely felt them. Instead, she was becoming more and more aware of something—or someone—with them in the forest. She felt eyes watching her from every direction, from behind each tree.

She squinted at the dark shapes and shadows around her. Had they moved?

Was it Blake? she wondered. Even though she had watched him leave, Abigail had a feeling that he wasn't gone.

Abigail and Cora kept moving, making their way deeper into the woods. They should have gotten to the creek by now, Abigail knew. But this part of the trail was rough and they needed to take their time.

On edge, Abigail began to concentrate more on the shadows around her and less on the trail. So when a root jutted up from the center of the pathway, she did not notice.

Abigail tripped over the root and fell into the dirt, face first. Though she did not cry out when she fell, the dirt that had been pushed into her face made her sneeze.

Abigail sneezed once, twice, three times before it was over.

The night noises, the snapping of small twigs, the rustling of leaves, which had been their constant companions along the path, stopped.

Abigail and Cora waited, not daring to move or speak. If someone was out there, they would have heard.

Suddenly, a branch snapped. In the silence of the night, it echoed loudly. Too loudly for it to have been made by a small animal, Abigail realized. Something was out there. It was big...and close.

Cora grabbed Abigail's arm, pulling her behind a bush. They crouched down, arms wrapped around each other.

Long seconds passed.

Then Abigail and Cora heard footsteps and the snapping of more twigs.

Abigail tried to get up to run but Cora held her there. She shook her head, a finger placed over her lips. If it was Blake, their only hope was to stay quiet.

He didn't know exactly where they were. It was dark. Maybe he'd even pass them by. If he got too close, then they would run. But they needed to wait and see.

The footsteps came closer.

Cora and Abigail moved toward the bush, hoping their dark clothing would keep them hidden.

Soon, the bush began to shake.

He was there, right on the other side...and making his way around to them.

Abigail pulled Cora to her feet. As the sound of footsteps came around the bush, Abigail opened her mouth to scream.

But a deer, not Thomas Blake, poked its head around the bush, chewing on leaves and berries.

Abigail and Cora were so surprised they said nothing for long moments. Then they laughed. And laughed. And laughed.

Chapter Fourteen
Maple Creek

Abigail and Cora continued along the path, not quite so worried now about the shapes, shadows, and noises around them.

"We'll be to the creek soon," Abigail whispered, hearing the rush of the moving water. "We'll have to move alongside it for just a little while. Then we can cross. This path will take us right to the spot."

Cora nodded. "Let's hurry."

They walked faster, anxious to reach their first goal.

"How long have we been gone?" Cora asked.

"I'm not sure. But it's taken us a lot longer than it should have. The path is smoother now, though. It will be easier to walk."

The sound of the water became louder. In her mind, Abigail pictured the creek. Though it was wide and rocky, the water usually ran slowly. There were some shallow parts near the banks that were fun for wading. Other parts were deep. Abigail was afraid of the deeper water and never went into it.

But as they arrived at the edge of the creek, it was not the slow-moving water Abigail had remembered. Instead, the stream was swift and swollen. Abigail and

Cora looked down from the steep bank to the black waters below.

"It's so high!" Cora exclaimed. "Will we be able to cross?"

"I don't know." Abigail shook her head. "I've never seen it like this before. That last thunderstorm...all the rain...What are we going to do?"

"First let's see if we can still cross."

They followed the path along the creek watching in silence as the water rushed by.

As they had made their way through the woods, the air had slowly gotten cooler. Now the wind picked up, bringing a chill to their skin. They both shivered. Even the extra protection of Will's clothing was not enough to keep them warm.

Suddenly, a faint rumble filled the air.

"Did you hear that?" whispered Abigail.

"It sounded like thunder," Cora answered, "but it was far away."

"I hope so."

Up ahead, the creek made a sharp bend.

"There it is," pointed Abigail. "That's where we cross."

They ran to the spot to which Abigail had pointed. But below them they saw only black water.

Abigail moaned. "It's too high! The rock bridge is completely under water."

"What if we follow the creek?" asked Cora.

"We'd have to walk along the road. But Isaac told us to stay away from roads...and people."

"I know," Cora agreed, "but there's nothing we can do. There is no way we can cross the creek now."

Chapter Fifteen
Along the Road

With the road winding to their left and the creek running swiftly and fiercely to their right, Cora and Abigail had only a small line of trees to keep them hidden.

Even so, this was the best place for now. For, across the road, there were open fields and pastures with barely a tree for safety. In those fields, if someone were to look closely, Abigail and Cora would be seen.

They walked cautiously, aware of every sound and shadow.

Suddenly, a stab of lightning lit the clouds. Only seconds later, a long rumble of thunder filled the air. There was no way to escape the storm, Abigail knew. With every step, they were heading straight into it.

* * * * *

Lightning struck with surprising flashes of light. Thunder rolled, a constant pounding that made the ground shake. The wind tugged at their hats and clothes. The storm was nearly there.

And then, along with the thunder, they heard something different. Quiet at first, but then louder. Horses.

They had been so distracted by the sounds of the storm, they hadn't heard the wagon coming up the road behind them. And it was coming fast.

With no place to hide, Cora pulled Abigail to the ground. They crawled behind the nearest cluster of tree trunks, then lay flat, hoping the darkness of the night and clumps of trees would hide them. And they waited.

The hoofbeats grew louder. The wagon roared up the road, past Cora and Abigail and around the next bend. Almost instantly, the hoofbeats blended into the sharp peals of thunder and then disappeared.

Abigail lifted her head and saw that Cora had done the same.

"Do you think it's safe?" Cora asked.

"We can't be sure," Abigail answered. "Stay here and I'll check. Don't move until I come back and tell you it's all right."

Cora nodded, then put her head back down.

Not far ahead, the road made its sharp turn, winding away from the creek. The trees were thicker there and as Abigail walked to the bend she felt safer knowing that she and Cora would be better hidden.

She listened—just the thunder and wind and the faint sound of rushing water. She watched. When the lightning lit the sky ahead she saw that the road was clear. The wagon had been moving quickly and was now out of sight.

Satisfied, she turned back, on her way to Cora, when out of the darkness, a hand, large and strong, grabbed her ankle.

Chapter Sixteen
Tricked

Thomas Blake let go of Abigail's ankle. He stood from the spot where he had been resting and stretched.

Shocked, Abigail stayed where she was, rooted to the ground. He'd caught her. She was going to go to jail and Cora would be sent back to her owner. She'd never see her mother again.

Lightning lit the sky. In the flash of light, Abigail saw Blake staring down at her. His hands were fisted on his hips, his legs spread wide. He was scowling.

"What are you doing out here all alone at this time of night, son?"

Son? Confused, Abigail said nothing. Then she understood. Abigail had forgotten she was wearing Will's clothes. In the darkness, Thomas Blake did not recognize her. He thought she was a boy.

"Answer me, boy!" Blake demanded. "What are you doing here?"

Thunder exploded in the sky and rumbled for long seconds, giving Abigail time to think.

She looked down at the ground, turning her face away from Blake. "My mama's very sick and Pa's taking care of her," she said, trying to make her voice sound like her brother's. "He sent me out to get the doctor. I need to hurry." Abigail turned to leave. She had to get away from him quickly before he realized who she was.

"Wait," Blake said. "I have a horse tied close by. I can take you to the doctor."

Not far away, Abigail saw his horse, tied to a low branch. As Blake untied it, Abigail's heart raced. She couldn't let him take her anywhere. But Blake would be suspicious if Abigail said "no". So what was she going to do?

Then she had an idea.

"Thank you, sir," Abigail said in her best male voice. "I am very tired."

Blake climbed up onto his horse and offered his hand to Abigail.

"We're not sure what Mama has," Abigail added, "but Pa won't let us near her."

Blake drew his hand back as Abigail reached out to take it. "Why not?" he asked.

"I don't know," Abigail said. She rubbed the back of her head, then her neck.

"What are you doing?" Blake demanded.

Abigail shrugged her shoulders. "I haven't been feeling well myself lately. Mister, you don't think Ma has smallpox or something, do you?" She pressed her hands against the small of her back and glanced up at him, a worried look on her face.

Even in the dark of night, Abigail could see Thomas Blake's eyes grow wide.

"Ah, sorry son," he said. "I forgot. I have to be in Jenkins' Falls. I took a little nap here by the road. I slept too long and now I'm late. I won't be able to give you a ride after all. But good luck."

Blake pulled sharply on the reins, dug his heels into the horse's side, and headed down the road.

Abigail watched him gallop around the bend and out of sight.

She ran back to Cora, breathless.

"What's wrong?" Cora asked.

"It was him. Thomas Blake. He grabbed me," she gasped.

"Thomas Blake? Thomas Blake was in the wagon?"

"No. He was taking a nap on the side of the road. He grabbed me while I was looking for the wagon."

Cora looked at Abigail's disguise and then her own. "He didn't recognize you?"

"No. He thought I was a boy." Abigail quickly told Cora what had happened.

"It's too dangerous to go any further by road, then," said Cora. "He may decide to come back."

"Then we have to cross the creek. Somehow. And, Cora, Thomas Blake is going to Jenkins' Falls, too."

Chapter Seventeen
Crossing the Creek

Farther on, the creek wound back into the forest. Abigail and Cora walked as quickly as possible alongside it, trying to find a way to cross. But as before, the water was too high and fast. It had risen well above any stepping stones that might have been lying in the rocky creek.

Lightning splintered the sky. Thunder boomed around them. Even through the trees, they felt the first hard splatters of rain. In seconds the splatters became a downpour, thick and cold.

Abigail spoke loudly in order to be heard above the storm. "Maple Creek winds back and forth from beginning to end. Even though it's going through the woods right now, it will take us back to the road eventually. We have to find a way to cross before it does."

It had been only minutes since the storm had begun but already Cora and Abigail were dripping. Lightning flashed above them. They walked slowly in the storm, searching the dark water for a way to cross.

"Look!" Cora exclaimed at last, pointing to the section of creek in front of them. She ran ahead pulling Abigail along.

In the flicker of the storm, Abigail saw it too. The creek was rather narrow here. A tree, tall and round, had fallen across it, from one side of the steep bank to the other.

Abigail looked at the tree. Then she looked at the rushing water below.

"This is it." She took a deep breath. "We have to cross here. It's our only choice."

Cora took her hand. "It will be all right. Just go slowly. And don't look down."

Cora stepped up onto the end of the tree, pulling her hat down snugly. "I'll go first," she told Abigail.

Cora took one careful step, placing her left foot in front of her right, arms out to her sides. She wobbled, then got her balance.

Another step and she was over the water.

Cora continued to move slowly across the fallen tree. With just a couple more steps, she disappeared into the darkness.

Abigail listened but heard nothing.

"Cora," she whispered loudly. There was no answer. "Cora?" she repeated.

"I'm fine," Cora whispered back. "I'm on the other side. It's your turn now." Lightning flashed. Through the sheet of rain, Abigail saw Cora standing on the other side of the creek.

"Be careful," Cora warned, "the bark is covered with moss. It's very slippery."

Abigail took a deep breath and stepped onto the tree trunk. The rain had made the tree's smooth bark slick. Abigail's foot slipped, causing her to lose her balance.

"Abigail?" Cora cried out.

"I'm all right." Abigail got back onto the log to try again.

This time, she placed her feet carefully. She held the knapsack out to one side, her other arm out to the opposite side to steady herself. Abigail moved her right foot in front of her left, heel to toe. And then again. One more step and she would be out over the black water. If she fell, she'd be carried away.

"Abigail," Cora said from the other side, "don't watch the water. You can do it if you keep your feet steady."

The storm raged on, making it difficult to see.

Abigail took another step and left the ground behind. She heard the fast-moving water below her. When a bolt of lightning lit the sky she looked straight ahead. Cora was waiting on the other side, waving her on. But she seemed so far away.

Abigail kept moving. She took her time, stopping after each step to keep her balance.

Suddenly the wind gusted. It pushed Abigail to her left. She waved her arms wildly, trying to keep her feet on the log. But her right foot slipped on the wet, moss-covered bark.

Abigail lost her balance. She twisted back and forth.

For one hopeful moment, she seemed to steady herself. But as she did so, Abigail dropped the knapsack from her hand. Seconds later it hit the water with a muffled plunk.

When Abigail looked down to see where it had gone, her foot slipped again.

She slid down the log, the tree scraping against her legs and stomach. Finally, her arms hit the trunk. Abigail wrapped one arm around it, holding tightly.

"Cora," she screamed. The lightning flashed. Abigail looked up, rain splattering her face. She saw Cora scooting across the log toward her.

"Cora, hurry!" she yelled.

Cora could see her now, hanging from the log. "Abigail, I'm here! I'm going to grab your arm and pull you up!"

"Hurry!" pleaded Abigail. "I can't hold on. I don't know how to swim!"

As Cora reached down to take Abigail's wrist, Abigail's hands slipped. She fell into the night.

"Abigail!" Cora screamed. There was no answer. Cora held on to the tree, looking down into the darkness, but Abigail had been swallowed by the black water.

"Abigail!" she screamed again. But all Cora heard was the rumble of thunder from above.

Cora jumped into the water.

Chapter Eighteen
Dark Water

As she fell, Abigail faintly heard Cora screaming her name. She wanted to yell back but then she hit the dark, cold water.

Abigail plunged down, deeper and deeper until she hit the rocky bottom.

When Abigail tried to push herself back to the surface, her foot became wedged between the rocks. She pulled at her foot but the rocks would not let her go. The swiftly moving water ripped the hat from her head and pulled at her clothing. The strong current pushed her down.

Suddenly she felt hands wrap around her chest. But though Cora pulled with all her might, Abigail's foot stuck fast.

Abigail's lungs burned. She didn't know how much longer she could hold her breath. Only seconds, she was sure. But Cora didn't give up.

Abigail felt Cora's hands move to her waist, then her legs. Cora wrapped an arm around Abigail's knees while she yanked and shoved at the rocks with her free hand.

Finally, Abigail felt the rocks shift. Cora grabbed Abigail's ankle and pulled her foot free.

In the instant the rocks released Abigail's foot, the girls paddled and kicked to the surface. With deep gasps they breathed in the cool air. But already the strong current had taken them far from the fallen tree. They coughed and gagged as the water dragged them under again and again.

Cora held on to Abigail tightly. She kicked and splashed, slowly working her way toward the edge of the creek.

Finally, as they came to a bend, Cora and Abigail brushed against the rocks close to the creek's edge.

"Put your feet down," Cora yelled above the roar of the current. "It's shallow here. We can stand if we try."

Like Cora, Abigail fought the current. Using each other as support, they stood. The water pushed and pulled at their legs, making the girls fall into the cold water again and again. But slowly, they made their way to the muddy bank.

Cora searched frantically for something to grab.

Just as the water began pulling them away once again, Cora's hand latched on to a small root. Though the water threatened to take them under, Cora held tight.

"Hold on to this root," Cora ordered, guiding Abigail's hand to the bank. "Try to climb up. There are more roots above this one."

Abigail grasped the root with her left hand and pulled herself into the bank. She reached out with her right hand and found another. The creek's bank was like a wall, high and steep. But inch by inch, she pulled herself higher, digging her feet into the mud.

Cora stood below, trying to keep her balance in the fast-moving water as she helped push Abigail to the top.

"I'm almost there." Abigail reached over the top of the creek's bank and pulled herself to safety. Then, still on her stomach, she turned around and looked back down over the edge.

Cora was already making her way up. When she was close enough, Abigail reached down and took Cora's arms. She pulled with all her strength until Cora was lying safely beside her.

Breathless and exhausted, Cora and Abigail lay on the ground, neither moving nor talking. They closed their eyes and let the raindrops wash the mud and grime away.

Chapter Nineteen
Another Life

Abigail knew that it must have been well past midnight. And their journey wasn't nearly over yet. They were running out of time. But they were cold, tired, and hungry. They had to find somewhere safe to rest, if only for a little while.

So Abigail and Cora got to their feet and followed the creek once again. Abigail wasn't sure how long they'd been in the water or how far the current had taken them, but at least they were on the other side now.

Though the thunder and lightning had faded, the wind still blew. It whistled through the treetops, making them sway back and forth. Cora and Abigail walked in silence, wet and shivering.

Slowly, through the darkness, Abigail began to recognize the area. The road would be coming up soon. Maple Creek was wide enough at this point to follow it for a little while longer.

Eventually, they passed the section of creek that wound close to the road and came once again to the fallen log. Abigail glanced at it quickly then turned away. She never wanted to see it again.

"I think it would be better now to go that way," Abigail said, pointing to the east and away from the creek. "Maple Creek leaves the road now, but winds back toward it later. We shouldn't risk staying so close to where someone could see us." Abigail ran her hand over her wet braids. "Especially since we lost our hats in the water."

Cora nodded in agreement.

As she turned to follow Abigail into the deep woods, however, her foot hit an object lying hidden in the darkness. Cora looked down and smiled. The book. Cora had left it on the bank beside the log for safe keeping when she'd gone back across to help Abigail.

Cora picked up the book and once again tucked it into the waistband of her trousers.

* * * * *

As they walked, the ground became rocky. Without a clear path to follow, they had to take each step carefully and try to keep moving in the same direction.

Finally, little by little, the wind blew the heavy clouds away. Every once in a while, through the trees, Abigail saw the full moon shining and a spattering of stars. The storm was over.

To Abigail's and Cora's relief, the forest became brighter as well. Most of the shadows disappeared. Tree trunks were simply tree trunks once again. Here and there, large rocks, ghostly white in the moon's light, lay scattered across the forest floor.

The ground rose higher. Weary, Abigail and Cora trudged up the hill.

"Look!" Abigail pointed. It was the first they'd spoken since the creek.

"What is it?" asked Cora.

"I think it's a cave."

Abigail and Cora rushed to the opening. Without a lantern they dared not go in, but they sat just inside its small opening, away from the chilling wind.

Since the food they'd brought had been lost in the creek, they sat, stomachs growling.

"I'm sorry about the biscuits, Cora," Abigail apologized.

"What do you mean?"

"I lost them in the water."

Cora shook her head. "It wasn't your fault. Besides, they were probably already ruined from the rain."

"I suppose so," Abigail agreed.

She sat quietly for a moment, then asked, "Cora, how long have you been running?"

Cora thought for a while, then shrugged her shoulders. "I'm not really sure, but at least a month, maybe more. After a while, the days start to run together. When you think back, it's hard to tell how many there were."

"Is it always like this? Like it is tonight?"

"Sometimes it's better. Sometimes it's worse. But it's always this scary. Isaac and I were always watching, always waiting for someone to jump out of the shadows. We never slept at night—always kept moving, through woods and fields and marshes, across streams and once, across a river. Sometimes we'd stay with someone, like we did at your house, but other times, we'd find a hiding place in the woods and try to sleep during the day until we could travel again at night."

"But how did you know which way to go?" Abigail asked.

"I didn't," said Cora. "But Isaac did. Sometimes he'd follow the North Star. Other times he'd check the tree trunks for moss to make sure we were going in the right direction. And he knew which towns to go to and which people would help." Cora wrapped her arms around her legs and rested her chin on her knees.

"Did you know that Isaac was a slave a long time ago?" Cora continued. "Just like me. In fact, he lived on the same plantation as my mother and me. I don't remember him well because he bought his freedom when I was very young. But I do remember that he was always nice to me. He used to tell me stories by the fire. Once, he told me that some day he would be free, too."

Abigail smiled. "And now he is."

"As we traveled north, Isaac told me about his life. He said that freedom was more than he'd ever imagined, but still it wasn't enough. He couldn't stop thinking about slavery. Finally, he realized that he had to help other slaves find freedom too."

"But how did he know how to do that?" asked Abigail.

"Have you ever heard of the Underground Railroad?"

Abigail shook her head.

"Isaac told me about it. The Underground Railroad is the name for a group of people who try to help slaves get to freedom.

"Some of the people, like Isaac, travel to the South to help slaves escape. They're called conductors. The slaves they take—like me—are called passengers. And the stops they make along the way are called stations."

"So my barn is a station?" asked Abigail.

Cora nodded.

"But how did you know that it would be safe?"

"Isaac has been a conductor for a long time. He knows where a lot of the stations are already. But even if he doesn't know the area, he can tell which people will help. A lot of times, stations will have certain signals to tell conductors that their place is safe. Like yours, some have a light burning in the top left window all night long. Others will have a chimney with one row of bricks painted white and still others may have a lantern with a different colored light burning in the window."

"Cora, did Isaac help your mother escape, too?"

"No. Isaac said that after I was sold to another plantation, Mama spent years asking about me. Finally, a slave who had been visiting the plantation said that he knew where I had been taken. After they spoke, my mother ran away on her own. As she went north, she found some people to help her. One person she talked to knew Isaac too. Through that person, Mama told Isaac where I was. She asked him to find me and bring me back to her so we could be a family again.

"She's supposed to stay here in Pennsylvania until I can meet up with her. Then we'll go on to Canada together."

"Cora, what would happen to you if you got caught?"

Cora was quiet while she thought of her answer.

"I don't know for sure," she said, shrugging her shoulders. "I've thought a lot about it, though. The slaves who try to escape and are brought back are punished.

"Sometimes they are given the hardest jobs on the plantation. Sometimes they are sold to another farm or plantation, away from everyone they know.

"When I was little, I can remember a group of slaves who tried to escape but didn't make it. When they were brought back, they were tied to a tree and whipped. The rest of us had to watch so that *we* would never try to escape."

Abigail closed her eyes, remembering the scars on Cora's back and legs.

"Were you ever whipped, Cora?"

Cora nodded and looked down at the ground.

"Why?"

"It was when I was younger," Cora answered, her voice growing quiet. "After they took me away from Mama..."

She stopped talking. Abigail looked over and saw the shine of tears in Cora's eyes. Wiping away her own tears, she put an arm around her friend. They sat in silence for a while longer, listening to the wind in the trees.

Finally, Cora spoke. "Since they made the new law in 1850, it's not safe for me anywhere in the United States. Not even in the North. Did you know that slave owners can capture runaway slaves wherever they're found, North or South? And now the Northern states have to help the slave owners.

"That's why we're going on to Canada. Plus," Cora continued, "anyone caught *helping* a slave escape can be punished. Isaac says that a lot of people are afraid to help now."

Abigail nodded. "The Fugitive Slave Act. Mama told me about it a little. I'm so sorry, Cora."

Cora looked at Abigail. "Don't be sorry. I'm cold and tired and hungry and scared, but I would do it again if I had to. Abigail, if I can find my mother and we make it to Canada, no one can ever make us go back to the plantation again. We'll be safe and we'll be free. And we'll finally be together.

"Come on," she said, pulling Abigail to her feet. "I want to make sure we're in Jenkins' Falls by morning. And from the color of the sky, we don't have much longer."

Abigail looked up through the treetops. The sky was no longer black. Cora was right. They still had over a mile or so to go. They had to hurry.

Chapter Twenty
Jenkins' Falls

It was easier now to see the rocks and roots along the forest floor. Abigail and Cora ran as quietly as they could. They ducked under low branches and jumped over the trunks of fallen trees that lay in their path.

Soon, the slope of the ground became steeper. They could no longer run, but Cora and Abigail didn't hesitate. Leaning forward, they used their hands and feet to climb the hillside, grabbing, pulling, and pushing their way up.

Out of breath, hearts thudding, they reached the top...and stopped cold in their tracks. Down the other side of the sloping hill, the forest gave way to an open meadow. Beyond the meadow stood a town, small and quiet in the shadows of early morning.

"That's it!" Abigail cried between breaths. "That's Jenkins' Falls!"

Cora's eyes grew big and round. She tore her eyes from the distant buildings and looked at Abigail.

"Are you sure?" she asked.

Abigail took her hand. "I'm sure. We're almost there."

They stood there a moment, looking out over the town.

"There's the road into Jenkins' Falls," Abigail pointed out. It lay to their left, stretching in easy curves until it met Maple Creek once again.

A small bridge crossed over the creek and then the road continued into town, splitting off in opposite directions.

Cora saw the clusters of buildings along the road and the dark shadows of houses dotting the land around it. Though the town was still quiet, some of the houses already glowed with light and had smoke rising from their chimneys.

"Where is the mill?" she asked.

Abigail pointed to the far end of Jenkins' Falls. "It's the big building way over to the left, right along the creek."

"But we'll have to go through town to get there!" Cora cried. "And it's going to be light soon. Someone will see us!"

Abigail shook her head. "We'll find a way." She wiped a hand at the beads of sweat that trickled down the side of her face and left a dark smudge of dirt.

"What about Thomas Blake?"

Abigail sighed. "He said he was headed here. We'll just have to hope that if he *is* here, we see him before he sees us."

Abigail pulled Cora down the steep hillside. "Let's go to that stand of trees on the other side of the meadow."

They half slid, half stumbled to the bottom, stopping at the edge of the woods. From here on they would be out in the open.

Abigail and Cora looked carefully across the meadow, then ran with all their might. Thorns and nettle jutted up from the ground at intervals and poked at their skin. The waist-high grasses, still wet from the heavy rain, slapped at their arms and legs.

At their fast pace, the ground beneath the grass was treacherous. It was riddled with bumps, dips, and holes. The girls tripped and slipped as they ran toward the safety of the trees.

Cora turned to look at Abigail. "We're almost there," she said. But as she turned back around, she stepped into a small hole.

With no time to react, Cora fell into the tall grass, twisting her ankle as she hit the ground.

Abigail saw Cora fall. When she didn't get up, Abigail ran to her side. Cora was lying on the ground, holding her ankle.

Abigail bent down and helped her up.

"Can you walk?" she asked.

Cora nodded, but yelled out in pain as she tried to take a step.

"What are we going to do?" Cora asked. She was so close and now this. She wanted to cry. But instead, she took another step. "Don't worry. I'll walk. Nothing is going to stop me."

"Come on," Abigail said, putting her arm around Cora to help her along. Together they limped toward the trees.

"Look," whispered Cora as they sat to rest her ankle under a large oak. Through the trees, they saw a small farmhouse.

Abigail helped Cora to her feet. They moved tree to tree, closer to the house.

From their new hiding place, Abigail could now see a barn through the pale morning light. Beside it, a wagon, loaded with sacks of grain, sat waiting.

Seconds later, a man walked out of the barn, leading a horse. Abigail and Cora watched silently as he hitched the horse to the wagon, then did the same with a second horse.

"Pa!" a voice yelled. A young boy came running from the other side of the house to the barn. "Pa! Ma said not to leave yet. You forgot your lunch."

The man bent down and scooped his son up into his arms. "Well thank you, Charles." He tousled the boy's hair and touched a finger to his small nose. "I was in such a hurry, I plum forgot."

They started off toward the house.

"Will you be gone long, Pa?" the boy asked.

"No. But I wanted to get an early start on the day. They're expecting these sacks of grain at the mill."

The father and son disappeared around the corner.

"Did you hear that?" Abigail asked. "He's going to the mill! You can't walk far, but if we could hide in his wagon..."

Abigail put her arm around Cora and walked her to the corner of the house.

"Stay here," she whispered. Abigail sneaked along the side to the opposite corner and peeked around.

The boy and his father were nowhere in sight. Now was their chance.

Abigail ran back to Cora. "It's safe...for now."

Cora held on to Abigail's shoulder tightly as they walked to the wagon.

Abigail helped Cora into the back, then climbed up herself.

Already, Cora was making a hiding spot. "Quick," she whispered from the corner, "come over here with me. I've found some empty sacks. We can cover ourselves with them."

She and Abigail curled up in the corner behind the sacks full of grain and pulled the empty sacks over their heads.

Moments later, the man climbed onto the wagon seat, whistling a cheery song. He snapped the reins and yelled, "Come on girls, the day's a waitin'!" to the horses.

With a jerk, the wagon rumbled forward.

Chapter Twenty-one
Wagon Ride

The ride on the small dirt road was rough. Abigail and Cora bumped and bounced in their cramped hiding space under the empty sacks. They held each other tightly, not daring to move or speak.

Abigail had no idea how far the wagon had traveled. But she could tell the man had the horses moving at a quick pace. The mill couldn't be far.

So what would they do once they got to the mill? How would they get out of the wagon without being seen? So caught up in her thoughts, Abigail barely noticed the sudden quiet. The man was no longer whistling.

"Hello there!" he yelled. After a few more feet, he pulled to a stop.

Abigail heard the sound of hoofbeats coming toward them. Her stomach twisted and churned. Had someone seen them climb into the wagon?

"I was wondering if you could help me?" a deep voice asked the man.

Abigail's skin tingled with nerves. She knew that voice. It was Thomas Blake.

Cora squeezed Abigail's hand. They were trapped.

"I'll help you if I can," said the man driving the wagon. "Are you lost?"

"No," said Blake with a snort. "I'm looking for a runaway slave named Cora—a young girl about fifteen years old. She might be with a man about your size."

Abigail heard the crinkle of paper as Blake showed the man a drawing and description of Cora.

"Nope. Haven't seen them around these parts," he said. "But I hope you catch 'em. You the owner?"

"No, just working for him. I'll be making my way around town, soon as more folks are up and about."

"Good luck. If I see them I'll be sure to let you know." With a loud snap of the reins, the wagon rumbled down the road again.

Cora's hand relaxed. Abigail felt herself relax too—just a little. They may have gotten away so far, but they weren't safe yet.

Soon the road became smoother. In minutes, they slowed and pulled to a stop.

The wagon shook as the man jumped to the ground. They heard his footsteps as he walked around to the back.

"Morning," another man said, approaching the wagon. "Got that grain for me today, I see."

"Yes, sir."

"Fine," said the other man. "I'll help you bring it in."

Abigail and Cora heard the back of the wagon being unlatched and pulled down. The men took one sack of grain from the pile, then another.

"You have a pretty good load here, John," the man said. "Go into the mill and stack them on the left. I'll grab another bag." From under the empty sacks, Abigail heard the men walk away from the wagon.

How many more sacks of grain were there? Abigail wondered, trying to remember.

She started to move, but heard the men coming back. More sacks were taken from the pile.

When they walked away again, Abigail peeked out of the wagon. In just the short time she and Cora had been hidden, the sky had lightened. They were running out of time. And they still had to find the house on the hill.

"We have to go now!" she whispered to Cora.

Hearts pounding, Abigail and Cora crawled out onto the ground and hid around the side of the wagon.

They waited one second. Two.

The men were still inside.

"Now!"

Abigail put her arm around Cora to help support her twisted ankle. Together, they limped as fast as they could past the horses and around to the side of the mill.

Abigail and Cora followed the building's stone wall to the back. Here, the mill stood at the edge of the creek where a giant wheel turned quickly in the rushing water. As it turned, it threw off a light mist that sprayed the girls' faces.

They looked ahead to the narrowed creek. A rickety rope bridge stretched across from one side to the other.

"Look!" Cora exclaimed. Across the creek, the ground rose in a grassy slope spotted with clumps of trees.

At the crest of the hill stood a white farmhouse. In the top left window a candle burned brightly.

Chapter Twenty-two
Sunrise

"Stay here," Abigail whispered. She ran back to the front of the building.

The men had unloaded the rest of the wagon and were standing beside it, talking. Abigail rushed back to Cora.

"They're at the wagon," she whispered into Cora's ear. "If we cross the bridge now, they won't see us."

The bridge was too narrow for Abigail and Cora to walk side by side, so Cora went first. They held on tightly to the bridge's ropes, swaying and bouncing with every step.

Abigail saw Cora wince with pain as she used her hurt ankle to cross, but Cora said nothing. She simply kept moving, never taking her eyes from the house at the top of the hill.

As soon as they were back on solid ground, Abigail helped Cora to the nearest cluster of trees. Suddenly, she noticed that the sky was light blue. How long had it been that way? She looked up and was surprised to see that the sun had already risen. After everything she and Cora had gone through to get there, they would be too late.

"Come on." Cora pulled on Abigail's arm.

"But Cora...the sun..." She pointed to the sky.

Cora shook her head. "Sunrise or not, it doesn't matter. I can't give up. Not now. Not when I'm so close." She let go of Abigail's arm and limped up the hill.

Abigail hesitated for a moment. But she knew Cora was right. She ran ahead to catch up with her friend. Together, they climbed the hill.

Chapter Twenty-three
So Close

Cora and Abigail carefully climbed the hill. They stopped every now and then, lying low in the tall grass to watch and listen. Finally they reached the top.

Abigail took Cora's hand. Her heart drummed as she gazed at the house in front of her. Cora would be free!

Suddenly, Cora pulled her down into the grass. "Listen!" she whispered before Abigail could speak.

She had been so happy to finally reach the house that Abigail had almost forgotten the danger. Now that she listened, she could hear it, too. Above the sound of the wind blowing through the tall grass she heard hoofbeats. At first, the sound was far away. But it was coming closer.

Abigail and Cora crawled further back into the grass. They lay flat on the ground and waited.

Though she couldn't see, Abigail heard the horse gallop up the road to the top of the hill. Then it came toward them and stopped in front of the house.

She heard the rider jump from the horse and walk quickly up the steps to the door. He knocked loudly three times. Then again.

When the door creaked open, Abigail strained to hear their voices. Though she could not hear much, she heard a man's voice and the words "fugitive slave." Her heart fell. Thomas Blake had beat them there.

Abigail heard a woman's voice next, then the door opened and closed.

Abigail cautiously peeked up over the grass. The porch was empty. The horse stood alone, grazing on the grass. Thomas Blake was inside the house.

Abigail squeezed Cora's hand. They had come so far. Cora had been so close to freedom. But they had nowhere to hide now. They had nowhere to go. Thomas Blake would find them.

Chapter Twenty-four
Footsteps

They lay on the ground for a long while, afraid to move or breathe. As they waited, the town behind them came to life. They heard faint shouts of "good morning!" and wagons being pulled along the road.

What would happen to them? wondered Abigail. Would Thomas Blake search the house as he had searched hers? Would he search the barn and property next? If so, where would they go? How would they ever get away?

Just then her thoughts were interrupted as the front door opened and slammed shut. They heard the sound of boots on the porch, then slow, heavy steps along the ground, coming closer.

Abigail held her breath, sure that Blake would hear it. She glanced at her friend. Cora's eyes were open wide with fear. A large tear rolled down her dark cheek.

Abigail gripped Cora's hand.

The footsteps stopped. Moving only her eyes, Abigail could see the brown of Blake's trousers a few feet away. But he had his back to her, looking down over the hill into town. He stood there, silent.

Suddenly, he turned and walked away. Abigail heard his horse whinny, then gallop back toward the road.

Chapter Twenty-five
A Friend with Friends

Abigail and Cora lay in the grass for a long while after, listening to the sound of the horse's hooves fade. When they could no longer hear the horse or any sound except for the town below, Abigail took a deep breath.

She got up slowly, carefully peeking out over the grass. Thomas Blake was indeed gone.

"Stay here," she whispered.

"No, I'll go," Cora argued. "It's dangerous."

"More dangerous if anyone sees *you* than *me*. Now stay here. I'll be all right. I promise." She gave Cora a sudden, fierce hug, then crept quickly to the front of the house.

She stopped and looked around once more. She was alone. Quietly, she walked up the steps to the porch and knocked.

The door opened only a crack. Abigail saw a woman peer out.

"Yes?" she asked.

Abigail simply stood at the door, all words escaping her.

The door opened further. A man and woman with kind eyes stood in the doorway. "I've not seen you around before," the man said. He looked at Abigail's wet braids, then at her boys' clothing. He knit his eyebrows. "Who are you, child?"

"A friend with friends," she said, barely above a whisper.

A look of relief flooded into the woman's eyes. "Where's the girl?" she asked.

"Hiding in the grass on the hill, until we knew it was safe."

"Go fetch her then. Quickly!" the woman ordered.

Abigail obeyed and when she and Cora got back to the porch, the woman took them inside and closed the door.

"I'm Mr. Henderson," the man introduced himself. "This is my wife. I'll go now to the barn and check on things while you get settled," he added and slipped outside.

"Don't worry. He'll make sure it's safe," said Mrs. Henderson. "Thank goodness you're all right," she sighed. "You almost didn't make it in time."

"But we did," said Abigail. "We did."

Chapter Twenty-six
Safety...At Last

Mrs. Henderson hurried Abigail and Cora into an upstairs bedroom.

"Help me push the bed to the left," she said. The girls pushed. Behind the headboard was a small door.

Mrs. Henderson opened it and went inside. Abigail and Cora followed. After Mrs. Henderson lit a lantern, the girls saw that the room was small and the ceiling low. But there were two soft feather mattresses and warm blankets.

"You may rest in here for a while."

She turned to Cora. "Mr. Blake is too close for you to start off right away. But don't worry, my husband will find some way to make up the time we've lost. Meanwhile, you can sleep...and eat. Biscuits and warm milk should make you feel better. Now let's take a look at that ankle."

* * * * *

With full stomachs, beds, and blankets, the girls slept comfortably. When Abigail woke, she saw in the dim light that Cora was sitting up, wrapped in a quilt.

"It almost seems like a dream, doesn't it?" asked Abigail. She rubbed her stiff muscles. "Or it would if it wasn't for all these aches and pains."

Cora laughed. "I'm sore too—especially my ankle."

Abigail got up and brought the lantern over to Cora's side. "The swelling has gone down," she said quietly. "In a few days it'll be fine."

Something lying in a dark shadow on the mattress between Cora and the wall caught Abigail's eye. She moved the lantern closer.

"The book! You still have it!"

Cora nodded, looking at the floor. "I hope you don't mind but I brought it along. I didn't put it in the knapsack. It was too important. I kept it with me instead."

"Of course I don't mind. I gave it to you for keeps. Did you read any of it while I was sleeping?" Abigail asked.

Cora did not answer at first. She looked at Abigail, then turned her head. "No."

Abigail shrugged her shoulders. "All right. I just thought it would help pass the time. Why don't we read some now?"

Abigail picked up the book. Though it had gotten damp in the rain, the pages were already drying.

"Go ahead," said Abigail. "We'll take turns reading it to each other. You can start." She handed the book to Cora.

Cora looked up at Abigail. A tear glimmered in her eye. "I would love to read, Abigail," she said slowly. "But I can't. I don't know how." She looked down at the book, tracing the cover lightly with her finger. Then she handed the book back to Abigail.

"Here," she said, "you can have it back."

"You don't know how to read?" Abigail asked. "Why?"

Cora took a deep breath, then admitted, "Slaves aren't allowed to learn how to read. It's against the law."

"But didn't you learn how to read in school?"

Cora shook her head. "I wasn't allowed to go to school, either."

Abigail let Cora's words sink in. "But you didn't say anything when I gave you the book."

"I didn't want you to know. And I've never had a book of my own. I wanted to pretend, at least for a little while, that I *could* read."

They sat together for a moment in silence. Then Cora said, "I've never even heard someone *read* a book other than the Bible."

Abigail put her arm around Cora's shoulders. She leaned close and whispered, "Then listen carefully..."

Abigail opened the damp pages and began to read.

* * * * *

Some time later, Mrs. Henderson knocked lightly on the door. She entered the small room with more food and water.

"I hope you've had a good rest."

When the girls nodded, she smiled. "Good. I've brought more food, so eat up. I also have a change of clothes for each of you. Then it's time to go. From what we could tell, Mr. Blake has traveled on now. It should be safe."

As Abigail and Cora ate, Mrs. Henderson chatted on and tended to Cora's ankle. She asked many questions about Isaac and their journey. "It's a brave thing you did." She looked at Cora, then Abigail. "Both of you."

"*Mostly* we were just scared to death," Abigail answered with a laugh.

"*Mostly* that's what bravery is," Mrs. Henderson said as she cupped each of their chins in a hand. "Going on with what needs to be done—even though you're scared.

"Now get dressed," she said with a laugh. "It's high time the two of you looked like girls again."

Chapter Twenty-seven
Goodbye

The wagon was ready. Mrs. Henderson went out to the barn with a basket of food for her husband while Abigail and Cora waited inside.

"I want you to have this." Abigail handed the book to Cora.

"But I told you...I can't read."

"Maybe not now. But soon you'll be in Canada. You'll be free. You'll be able to go to school and learn to read and write. Maybe someday it will be your favorite book, too."

"It already is." Cora took the book and hugged Abigail fiercely. "I'll never forget you."

With tears in her eyes, Abigail hugged her in return and smiled. "I'll miss you, Cora."

After Abigail and Cora said goodbye, Mrs. Henderson took Cora out to the barn.

Not long after, the barn doors opened. Mrs. Henderson waved goodbye as Mr. Henderson drove away in the wagon, a basket of food on the seat beside him. There was no sign of Cora.

Abigail panicked. "Cora! What about Cora?" she burst out when Mrs. Henderson came back inside.

"She's safe."

"But I didn't see her."

"Of course not. You're not supposed to. No one is supposed to. Don't worry. Cora is in the wagon in a secret compartment that was made for just this reason. She's hidden very well. No one will find her."

She looked at Abigail and took her hands. "Well now," she said, "it's time that you start back too. Your mama will be waiting."

Chapter Twenty-eight
The Letter

Eight months later...

Abigail fed Nathan, her baby brother, by the fire as the cold rain poured down outside. Her mother was busy making stew for supper. Will sat at the table doing homework.

A wagon pulled up. Abigail watched at the window as her father put the horse in the barn, then ran to the house, a smile on his face.

Abigail opened the door.

"What is it, Pa?" she asked.

"Oh, nothing much," he said with a shrug of his shoulders. "Just this." Pa opened his coat and pulled out a white envelope.

"A letter?"

"Not just *a* letter," Pa said as he hung his wet hat and coat and sat down by the fire. "A letter for *you*."

"For me!" Abigail's face lit up. She handed her brother to Pa and grabbed the letter. "I've never gotten my own letter before. Who's it from?"

"I don't know. Open it and see!" her pa laughed.

Abigail ran to her room, tearing open the envelope as she went. She jumped onto her bed and unfolded the letter.

The writing was large and shaky. But she could tell the writer had taken great care to form the letters correctly. She read:

Dear Abigail,

> *I made it! I'm free!*

> *We crossed the border into Canada two weeks after the Hendersons. It was a long ride, but worth every second. I'm with my mother now. She's wonderful. She's as beautiful as I remembered. And she loves me. She really loves me. She cried the whole first day we were together.*

> *I'm allowed to go to school here, just like you said. I'm learning to read and write. In fact, this is my very first letter. Mama helped me a little (she's learning to read and write, too) and so did my teacher. I wanted to get everything just right.*

> *The book you gave me is my favorite. The words are hard because I'm still learning, but my teacher says that I am reading better every day. I practice all the time!*

> *Please write back and tell me all about what's happened since we left each other. How did you get back home? Have you seen Thomas Blake again? How is Isaac? Please say that he is all right.*

> *I miss you, Abigail.*
> > *Love,*
> > *Cora*

Abigail read the letter over and over. Then she took out a pencil and paper.

Dear Cora...

Chapter Twenty-nine
A New Abigail

The next morning, Abigail woke early. She braided her hair and dressed quickly. The smell of bacon and biscuits made her stomach rumble.

She ran down the steps to the kitchen.

"Good morning, Abigail," called her brother. He was eating a breakfast big enough for two.

"Morning, Will," she replied, stopping to snatch a biscuit from the table. "Morning, Nathan." She stooped over and gave her baby brother a kiss. "Where are Ma and Pa?"

"In the barn. Sit down and have some breakfast."

"I will later...if there's any left," she added, looking at his plate. "I have chores to do before school."

"Mine are already done."

Abigail wrinkled up her nose at him, but said nothing. She grabbed the lantern, then turned and walked out the door.

The morning was still very dark but Abigail took no mind of it. She pulled her cloak tightly around her shoulders and walked to the barn.

Old Bessie was already getting noisy.

"Oh, Bessie, I'm coming," Abigail scolded as she opened the barn door.

She walked quickly over to Bessie's stall.

"Quiet now, girl," she whispered, rubbing the old cow's ears.

With gentle strokes and soft words, Abigail calmed her. Then the barn was silent. Abigail held up the lantern and glanced about. Ma and Pa were nowhere in sight.

With a smile, Abigail walked to the corner of the stall. The hay had been cleared away. After one last look around the dark barn, she bent down and knocked on the loose floorboards. She moved them to the side and looked into the hidden room below.

As she peeked over the edge, she saw frightened faces looking back up at her. A small group of slaves was huddled in the corner—two men and a woman. Abigail's mother and father were giving them food and warm blankets.

In the other corner, holding a small, sleeping child, sat Isaac.

Isaac didn't speak, but he smiled and winked. Abigail winked back, then replaced the floorboards and finished her chores.

Educational Resources

Glossary

conductor. Person who guides slaves north toward freedom on the Underground Railroad.

fugitive slave. Runaway slave.

Fugitive Slave Act of 1850. The second fugitive slave act passed to protect slavery; harsher than the first, it required officials to arrest suspected slaves, holding the officials liable to a $1000.00 fine if they refused. This second act also gave Federal marshals the right to search any home for fugitives; anyone discovered aiding a fugitive slave could be imprisoned for 6 months or fined $1000.00.

passenger. Runaway slave traveling along the Underground Railroad.

station. A safe place along the Underground Railroad where slaves/conductors could rest, receive food, clothing, and possibly medical attention. Some of the more frequently used stations included barns, attics, cellars, hidden rooms, dry wells, and churches.

stationmaster. Person responsible for the station and its provisions.

Underground Railroad. Secret system of escape routes used by slaves to find their way north to freedom.

The Underground Railroad

The African slave trade was introduced to the American colonies in the 1600s. Taken from their homes and families, the slaves were bought and sold as property. As such, the slaves could not vote, own land, or learn to read and write. Even marriage between slaves was not legally binding and could be dissolved at any time. In addition, work, rest, food, and discipline—which could range from mild to severe— were based upon the owner's wishes. The slaves had no control over their own lives.

Living under such conditions, many slaves escaped to the North. In 1793, therefore, Congress passed the first Fugitive Slave Law. This law gave slave owners (and slave catchers) the legal right to cross state lines to capture a fugitive slave. The owner needed only to present proof of ownership to a judge. The slave, on the other hand, did not have the right to speak on his or her own behalf. In addition, anyone found aiding a fugitive could be fined $500.00.

The Fugitive Slave Law of 1793 was not fully enforced in the North, however, and the tensions between the North and the South grew. By the 1800s, abolitionist groups had begun to loosely organize a system of escape routes to aid fugitive slaves in their quest for freedom. This system eventually became known as the Underground Railroad (a name coined around the 1830s).

Because assisting fugitive slaves was illegal, however, members of the Underground Railroad worked in secrecy. In order to help preserve this secrecy, they used code words—based on the idea of a railroad—to communicate with one another. Some of these terms included *passenger*, *conductor*, *station*, and *stationmaster*.

As part of the Underground Railroad, the conductor journeyed south to help one or more passengers (slaves) escape. For weeks/months, the conductor and passengers traveled under the cover of darkness by a variety of methods: foot, wagon, boat, horse, or even train.

On their way north, conductors and passengers stopped at stations (safe houses) to receive food, clothing, and rest as well as any needed medical attention. Stations—usually 10-20 miles apart—included such places as attics, cellars, barns, churches, dry wells, and secret rooms.

Stationmasters (people providing the stations and provisions) let conductors know a station was safe through secret signals such as a light in the upper, left window, a flag in the hand of a statue, or a row of painted, white bricks on a chimney.

Southern slave owners were upset by the North's apparent lack of assistance to help them capture their slaves. In fact, some Northern citizens even fought the slave owners' efforts. In 1850, therefore, at the urging of Southern slave owners, Congress passed a second, more severe, Fugitive Slave Law. This second law *required* officials to capture suspected fugitive slaves.

If an official refused, he could be fined a sum of $1000.00. In order to claim the slave, the owner merely had to show proof of ownership to a commissioner. A commissioner ruling in favor of the slave received a $5.00 payment; one siding with the slave owner received a payment of $10.00. In addition, this law also gave Federal marshals the right to search anyone's home for suspected fugitives. A person discovered aiding a fugitive, in this manner or any other, could be imprisoned for six months and/or fined $1000.00.

Due to the stronger provisions of the Fugitive Slave Law of 1850, the Northern states were no longer a safe haven for fugitives. Many slaves continued the long and perilous journey farther north into Canada.

Instead of halting the Underground Railroad as was intended, the Fugitive Slave Law of 1850 only succeeded in increasing its supporters. In fact, the 1850s were the most active time period in the Underground Railroad's history.

To travel along the Underground Railroad required great courage. Those who attempted the journey had to leave family, friends, and all that they knew (many having been born into slavery) with only the hope and faith that they would reach freedom and begin a new life.

In addition, the journey north was perilous. Fear, exhaustion, hunger, and the threat of capture were constant companions. Slave owners, wanting to reclaim their "property," advertised rewards for capture and employed merciless slave catchers and bloodhounds to track them down.

When slaves *were* captured, punishments could be brutal. While some slaves were forced to wear chains and irons, others were sold to another plantation, possibly farther south. More violent punishments ranged from severe beatings and whippings, maiming, branding, and, in some cases, death. But, possibly, worst of all, was the slave's knowledge that he or she had been so close to freedom just to have that freedom taken away.

Regardless of its perils, however, the Underground Railroad offered decades of hope and new life for those who wanted freedom so badly. It is estimated that approximately 100,000 slaves found their way north through its secret channels.

The Underground Railroad remained active until the end of the Civil War when the Union was once again reunited. In December of that same year, Congress ratified the 13th Amendment, legally ending the long-standing institution of slavery.

Lesson Plan
The Underground Railroad

Vocabulary and Facts

Objective: Students will:
- ◆ identify the roles of: conductor, passenger, station, and stationmaster
- ◆ identify two or more facts learned about the Underground Railroad

Materials: construction paper railroad ties and rails; a set of four index cards (with the terms *passenger*, *conductor*, *stationmaster*, *station*) per student; prepared list of descriptors for the terms *passenger*, *conductor*, *stationmaster*, *station*; non-fiction Underground Railroad book.

Procedure:
1. Have students imagine they are slaves in the 1850s. Discuss conditions of slavery life. Tell the students to pretend that they want to escape to the North where they can live freely. How would they do so? (Show location of their plantation on a map and where they have to go.) Discuss ideas about direction, travel, food and water, rest, and most importantly, avoiding capture.

2. Briefly describe the Underground Railroad and its role in helping slaves escape to freedom.

3. Read non-fiction book that focuses on the Underground Railroad.

4. Discuss terms (passenger, conductor, station, stationmaster).

5. Discuss signals, methods and techniques of conductors and stationmasters to keep passengers safe.

6. Hand each student a set of four index cards. Using the prepared list of descriptors, call out a descriptor and have the students raise the card that fits the description (example descriptor: traveled south to help slaves escape).

7. Hand out at least two construction paper railroad ties per student. The students write one fact they learned about the Underground Railroad on each tie.

Closure: Tape rails to the classroom wall or other acceptable area, with the word "slavery" on one end of the tracks and "freedom" on the other. Students share facts as a class then tape them along the rails, beginning at the "slavery" end. As students learn more about the Underground Railroad they may add more ties and eventually reach "freedom."

Lesson Plan
Midnight Journey

Character Comparisons

Objective: The students will:
- ◆ brainstorm traits of *Midnight Journey*'s characters
- ◆ discuss choices, citing examples from text
- ◆ compare and contrast character traits using a Venn diagram

Materials: copies of Venn diagrams, one copy per group; *Midnight Journey*; optional—a second fictional book of students' choice

Procedure:

1. Teacher reviews *Midnight Journey*'s plot and characters with students. As a whole, the class will hold a brief discussion in which students may name a favorite character and reasons supporting that choice.

2. The teacher creates a Venn diagram, each section labeled with a character from *Midnight Journey*.

3. As a class, the students brainstorm traits of each character (physical, emotional, etc.), citing examples from the text. The teacher and students then compare and contrast the characters by

listing the traits into the appropriate Venn diagram sections.

4. Discuss results.

5. In small groups, the students choose two (not same two) of *Midnight Journey*'s characters to compare. Label sections of Venn diagram with characters' names. Students discuss character traits, citing examples from the text. They next compare and contrast the characters by listing the traits in the appropriate sections of the Venn diagram.

Optional: Students compare and contrast one character from *Midnight Journey* with a character from a different fictional book. Follow same steps.

Closure: As a whole class, students discuss small group choices.

Discussion Topics

◆ Ethical nature of slavery

◆ Rights of slave owners vs. slaves

◆ Impact of the Underground Railroad on American/ African American history

◆ Important figures of the Underground Railroad— identify, describe their roles in the Underground Railroad as well as their impact on slavery

◆ If students were to put themselves in the role of a slave in the 1850s, would they have tried to escape along the Underground Railroad? Why or why not?

◆ If students imagined themselves as a free person in the 1850s, would they have participated in the Underground Railroad? Why or why not? If so, what role would they have assumed?

◆ Role of herbal remedies in the 1800s

Classroom Activities

◆ On a United States map, trace the routes of the Underground Railroad

◆ Students research and discuss an herbal remedy, its uses, and how it was prepared

◆ Students assume the role of Cora; write a diary entry for the rest of her journey into Canada

◆ Students assume the role of Abigail; write a diary entry of her feelings about one of the following: helping Cora; Thomas Blake; her mother; Isaac; how Abigail thought she'd changed after becoming part of the Underground Railroad

◆ Students discuss and draw pictures of what the story means to them (not plot or characters) using words, symbols, colors, etc.; share with the class

Selected Bibliography

Bial, Raymond. *The Underground Railroad*. Boston: Houghton Mifflin Company, 1995.

Carson, Mary Kay. *The Underground Railroad for Kids: From Slavery to Freedom*. Chicago: Chicago Review Press, 2005.

Geocities. "A Union Forged in Chains." *The Fugitive Slave Laws*. http://www.geocities.com/Athens/Agora/3992/Lesson1/index.html (accessed March 14, 2006).

Henry, Matthew. "Fugitive Slave Laws." Richland College of the DCCCD. http://www.rlc.dcccd.edu/annex/COMM/english/mah8420/FugitiveSlaveLaws.htm (accessed March 14, 2006).

Hoskins, Jim. *Get on Board: The Story of the Underground Railroad*. New York: Scholastic, Inc., 1993.

Stein, Conrad. *The Story of the Underground Railroad*. Chicago: Children's Press, 1981.